Sea

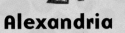
Alexandria

Giza

Cairo

Y

P

T

ISRAEL

JORDAN

SAUDI
ARABIA

River Nile

Luxor

Kom Ombo

Red Sea

For Valérie and Eric Vialet-Douay
and their children Pauline, Laura and Antoine

Riddle of the Nile copyright © Frances Lincoln Limited 2006
Text and illustrations copyright © Deborah Nash 2006

First published in Great Britain in 2006 and in the USA in 2007
by Frances Lincoln Children's Books, 4 Torriano Mews, Torriano Avenue, London NW5 2RZ
www.franceslincoln.com

Distributed in the USA by Publishers Group West

British Library Cataloguing in Publication Data
available on request

ISBN 10: 1-84507-466-1
ISBN 13: 978-1-84507-466-1

Illustrated with sand from Egypt, tissue paper,
oil pastel, watercolour, acrylic paint, glitter and gold foil

Set in Base Nine and Walcome One

Printed in China
1 3 5 7 9 8 6 4 2

RIDDLE
OF THE NILE

Deborah Nash

FRANCES LINCOLN CHILDREN'S BOOKS

Winding down the River Nile were two crocodiles, one big, one small. Baby Crocodile caught up with Crookedy Crocodile and snapped, "One day I shall be King of the Nile!"

"Oh yes?" grinned Crookedy Crocodile. "You'll have to prove yourself first ..."

"What do I have to do?"

"Answer this riddle," cracked Crookedy Crocodile.

"As I was on my way to Cairo
I met a man who was a Pharaoh.
This Pharaoh had seven servants,
Each servant had seven sacks,
Each sack had seven cats,
Each cat had seven kits.
Kittens, cats, servants, sacks –
How many were going to Cairo?"

"I don't know," replied Baby Crocodile.
"If you want to be King of the Nile,
you'd better find out," snickered Crookedy Crocodile.
And away he swam.

There were once many crocodiles in Egypt, but now they are found mainly in Lake Nasser. Ancient Egyptian fishermen used water spells to keep crocodiles away from their boats. Today, crocodiles are in danger from people who hunt them for their skins.

"Snap! Snap!" went Baby Crocodile.
"It's a tricky puzzle. I'll ask the
Great Sphinx at Giza — he might know."
Baby Crocodile crawled out of the water
and down the busy streets.

He found the Sphinx sitting in the shadow of the Pyramid of Khafre and recited the riddle to him.

"I'm not as sharp as I was," confessed the Sphinx. "I'm thousands of years old. All I know is that I'm smaller than the pyramid behind me and bigger than the camel in front..."
And the Sphinx fell asleep.

The Great Sphinx is made from limestone. He has the body of a lion and the head of a man. Some people think that the Sphinx's head is a portrait of Pharaoh Khafre whose pyramid he guards.

Baby Crocodile sneezed as the sand got up his nose.
He told the riddle to a cobra curled up by a pyramid,
but the cobra hissed, "Come back next week,
next month, next year! Then I'll have the answer."
  But Baby Crocodile didn't want to wait that long.

The pyramids at Giza were built on the west bank
of the Nile. The Ancient Egyptians believed that
this was the place where the Kingdom of the Dead
could be found.

So he swam along the Nile until he reached a Nilometer carved on a stone wall.

"One, two, three, four..." counted the frog who was guarding it. Baby Crocodile told him the riddle.

"All I know," croaked the frog, "is that my Nilometer measures the water level of the Nile." And away he hopped.

The Nilometer was invented by the Ancient Egyptians to record the rise and fall of the river each year. If the water level was high, the farmers were asked to pay more tax because they knew the harvest was going to be good.

Baby Crocodile pondered the riddle as he paddled down the river. He saw one aeroplane, two mosques, three water-wheels, five people and eight palm trees. Then the sun sank and it was night.

Water-wheels help to irrigate the fields by lifting water from the canals which join the river.

Mosques were built by the Arabs who invaded Egypt in AD 642, bringing the religion of Islam with them. Most Egyptians are Muslims.

Baby Crocodile swam on, singing softly to himself:

"As I was on my way to Cairo
I met a man who was a Pharaoh..."

"I know who that was!" interrupted a Nile perch.
"But do you know the answer?" asked Baby Crocodile.
"Of course," bubbled the perch, but before
he could say it, a cat with golden eyes caught the fish
and gobbled him up.

Fish is often used in Egyptian cooking.
Sayadia is a fish stew served with rice.
The Nile perch and the tilapia were eaten
by people in Ancient Egypt and they are
still caught and cooked today.

"Seven times seven times seven times seven..."
sang seven papyri growing along the banks of the river.
"Do you know the answer?" asked Baby Crocodile.
"No," they whispered. "But there's a library
at Alexandria. You might find it there."

Papyrus is a plant that once grew on the
banks of the Nile. It was made into scrolls
by the Ancient Egyptians. Nowadays, tourists
buy paintings on papyrus as souvenirs.

When Baby Crocodile arrived in Alexandria,
he was amazed at the size of the library.
He crept round it one way and then back the other way.
In the courtyard, a statue of Alexander the Great
watched him.
"Crocodiles are not allowed in the library," he said stonily.
"But there's something I need to find out,"
pleaded Baby Crocodile.
"The answer is simple and you
won't find it here. Go back
to the Nile," commanded
the statue.

When Alexander the Great invaded Egypt, he built a city
called Alexandria in 331 BC. A great library was set up
there. It was destroyed by fire, but today there is
a new library. It looks like a huge discus and can hold
eight million books.

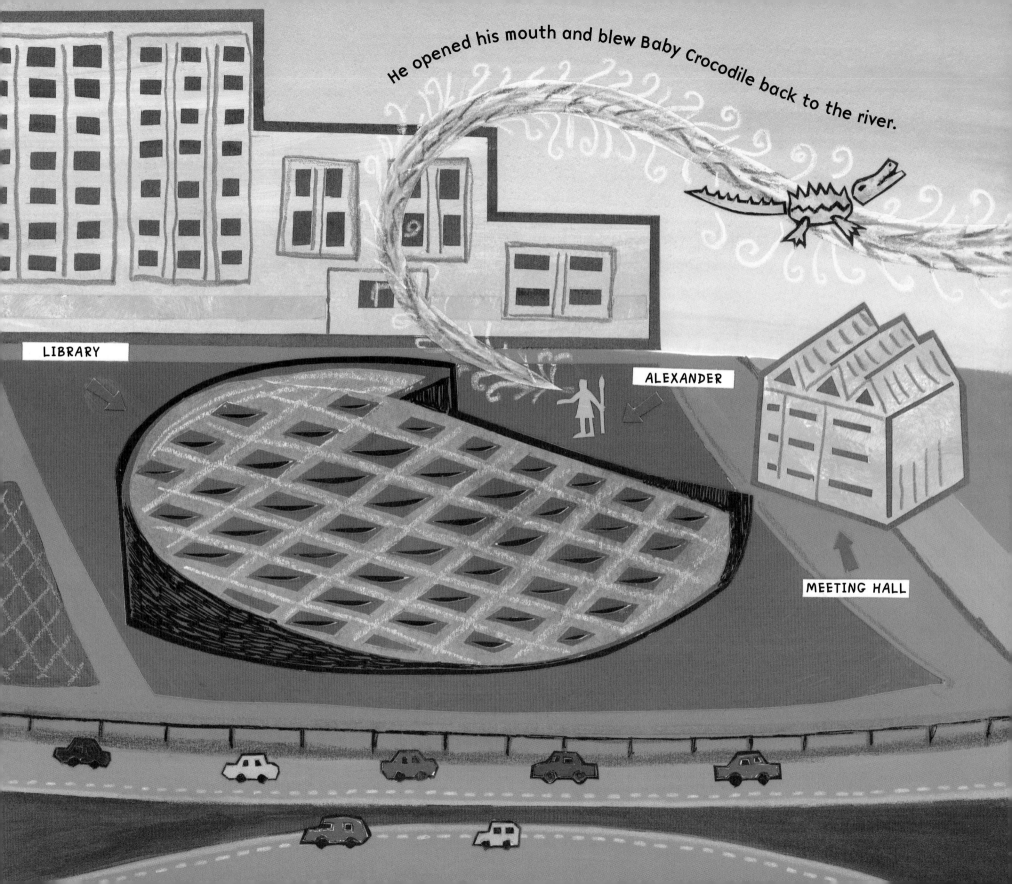

Baby Crocodile swam on until he came to a museum.
He decided to rest and take a look inside.
There were all kinds of animals wrapped up in linen
bandages – a cat, a bull and even a baby crocodile
like himself. He was sad when he saw this,
and crawled back to the Nile.

Ancient Egyptians mummified their favourite
pets and the sacred animals they worshipped.
Animals were also mummified as food for
the Pharaohs in the afterlife. "Mummy brown"
was a brown paint made from the ground
bones of mummies. Up to the 19th century,
artists used it in their paintings.

Then he met a fisherman in his boat.
"Keep away, crickety-crackety crocodile," cried the fisherman,
"or you'll frighten the fish and I won't catch any."
"But I'm only a baby!" glugged Baby Crocodile.
"You don't look like a baby to me,"
bellowed the fisherman – so loudly
that the Ba Bird heard him.

The Ba Bird was painted
on the walls of Ancient Egyptian tombs
and represented the human spirit.
It had the body of a bird and the head
of the person who had died.

"*Caw! Caw!*" called the Ba Bird. "What's up, Croc?"

"I want to be King of the Nile," blubbered Baby Crocodile, "but I've got to answer a riddle first." And he repeated the rhyme.

"It's a very odd riddle," said the Ba Bird, "and it's something to do with the number seven. I'll go up to heaven and find out."

The Sky Goddess of the Ancient Egyptians was painted as a giant woman with stars on her body who bends over the world. She swallows the sun each evening and gives birth to it again the next morning.

So the Ba Bird flew up to heaven where
the Sky Goddess Nut was watching over the world.
"Tell Baby Crocodile to visit Sobek
the Crocodile God," she murmured.

Baby Crocodile swam slowly down to Kom Ombo.
There, in his secret temple, lived Sobek, the colossal
Crocodile God. Baby Crocodile trembled when he saw him.

"Who are you?" thundered Sobek.

"I'm Baby Crocodile."

"Hmm. You're quite big for a baby."

It was true. Baby crocodile had grown during his search.
He was now a Big Crocodile.

Big Crocodile cleared his throat and recited the riddle.

"As I was on my way to Cairo
I met a man who was a Pharaoh.
This Pharaoh had seven servants,
Each servant had seven sacks,
Each sack had seven cats,
Each cat had seven kits.
Kittens, cats, servants, sacks –
How many were going to Cairo?"

The temple at Kom Ombo is dedicated
to two gods: Sobek, the crocodile god
and Horus the Elder, the falcon-headed god.
It has a pool where sacred crocodiles were
once kept. An adult Nile crocodile grows to
an average length of 5 metres (16 feet 4 inches).

"There is only one simple answer
to that riddle," boomed Sobek.
    And in a flash, Big Crocodile knew
the answer. He looked up at the sun.

The Ancient Egyptians worshipped the sun
as the bringer of light and life. They gave the sun
different forms — a man with a falcon's head
and sun disc, a sun with rays like outstretched hands,
or a scarab beetle rolling the ball of the sun.

"*Hamdu lillah!* There is only one sun in the sky and only one answer. The answer is one! Only one was going to Cairo. Everyone else was going the other way!"

Big Crocodile grinned. As he turned towards the river, a crown of lotus flowers appeared on his head.

Now at last he really was King of the Nile!

Hamdu lillah means "Thanks be to God" in Arabic.

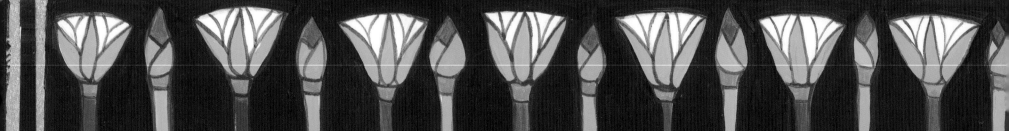

The world's oldest mathematical document is the Ancient Egyptian Rhind papyrus. It has a riddle like this one with seven houses, seven cats, seven mice and seven ears of spelt (a kind of wheat).

The Pyramid Fortune Game

Baby Crocodile would like playing this game to guess his fortune.
You can play it too — it's great fun and easy to make.

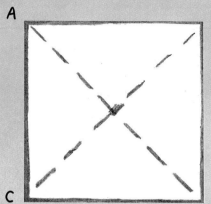

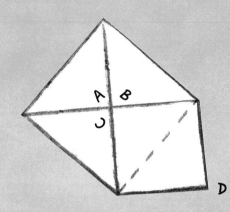

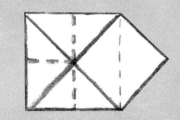

1. Begin with a 21cm x 21cm ($8^{1}/_{4}$ ins x $8^{1}/_{4}$ ins) square of thin paper.

2. Fold corner A to corner D to make a crease. Unfold, then fold corner B to corner C. Unfold. Your square paper will now have two diagonal creases.

3. Fold each corner to the centre of the square to make a smaller square. Turn the paper shape over.

4. Fold the new corners to the centre of the square to make an even smaller square.

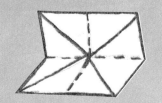

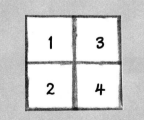

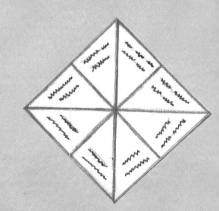

5. Fold the new square in half in both directions.

6. Turn over, and number the square flaps as above. Turn over.

7. Draw the pictures shown on the next page on the triangular flaps.

8. Open the flaps and write the meaning for each picture inside.

How to play the Pyramid Fortune Game

1. Hold *the* pyramid fortune-teller with a finger and *thumb* in each of the square pockets.

2. Ask a friend to choose one of the numbers shown.

3. Count out the number by opening and closing the fortune-teller.

4. Ask your friend to choose one of the pictures shown.

5. Spell out the name of the picture (for example C-A-T) by opening and closing the fortune-teller.

6. Then choose another picture. Open the flap for *that* picture and read your friend's fortune.

A cat
You are gentle and friendly.

A cobra
You always protect others.

A crocodile
You are creative and fierce.

A frog
You will *have* a lot of children.

A lotus
You love life.

A papyrus scroll
You are very knowledgeable.

A scarab
You are sacred like the sun.

A wadjet eye
You are powerful and all-seeing.

LIBYA

E   G